STEP BROTHER
with Benefits

MIA CLARK

Book design by Cerys du Lys
Cover design by Cerys du Lys
Cover Image © Depositphotos | avgustino

Cherrylily.com

DEDICATION

Thank you to Ethan and Cerys for helping me with
this book and everything involved in the process.
This is a dream come true and I wouldn't have been
able to do it without them. Thank you, thank you!

CONTENTS

ACKNOWLEDGMENTS

Thank you for taking a chance on my book!

I know that the stepbrother theme can be a difficult one to deal with for a lot of people for a variety of reasons, and so I took that into consideration when I was writing this. While this is a story about forbidden love, it's also a story about two people becoming friends, too. Sometimes you need someone to push you in your life, even when you think everything is fine. Sometimes you need someone to be there, even when you don't know how to ask them to stay with you.

This is that kind of story. It is about two people becoming friends, and then becoming lovers. The forbidden aspects add tension, but it's more than that, too. Sometimes opposites attract in the best way possible. I hope you enjoy my books!

STEPBROTHER WITH BENEFITS

1 - Ethan

Yeah, YEAH, I know what you're thinking. Ethan, why are you such an asshole? Don't be such a prick, dude. Ashley just wants to hang out with you. She's your stepsister so you can be friends with her, right?

Yeah, well, listen up. Do you ask a cat why it's a cat? Do you go around asking the cat why it chases mice or red laser dots? Hey, cat, why the fuck did you just knock that piece of paper off the table? Stupid cat.

That's just what cats do. They don't give a fuck what you think, and asking a cat to stop doing the things that every cat in the entire world does is not only stupid, it's useless as fuck. The cat's just going to keep doing it, so what's the point.

I'm an asshole and a prick and a cocky, arrogant bastard, so I don't know why you want me to change all of a sudden. I've been like this for awhile now. Ashley knew what I was before she tried to get involved with me, and she should know what I am now that we're back to the basics. It is what it is. I can't change the world.

I just fucking... I don't want to deal with this shit right now. I need to get away. I need to get my mind off of everything. I can't be around her right now. I get in the car and I drive off and leave her there. At home.

Our home. I have to go back sometime, don't I? Well, fuck. Fuck fuck fuck.

Maybe not. Maybe I can get a hotel room or something. Just chill there. Oh yeah? And how long should I plan on doing that? The entire summer, I guess. She's not going anywhere. If I don't want to see her again, I'd have to take some serious drastic action.

Vacation maybe? I'm sure I could find someone to hang out with. Go chill somewhere nice. Cancun or Jamaica or whatever the fuck. Where's that Hedonism place? Yeah, the one where people just do whatever they want, fuck around, giant orgies, walk around naked, who cares? I've never been, but if anything can get me to stop thinking about Ashley, it's that place.

Or, why do I have to stop thinking about her? Vacation? Yeah, well, shit. Let's go! Me and her. Aruba is nice. Mostly old people vacationing there. I've been a few times. That makes it perfect, though. We can do whatever the fuck we want for the entire summer. We could walk around and hold hands, cuddle out in the open, kiss on the beach while the sun sets, and no one would ever have to know she's my stepsister. It wouldn't matter. No one would even think to ask.

Yeah, well, that's not going to work. Not after the shit I just pulled. Can't even be bothered to study with her, treat her like shit in front of our parents, and then what? I'm going to go back there and say I'm sorry and ask if she'll spend our summer break on some exotic island with me? Kind of suspicious, don't you think?

Yeah...

I don't know where I'm going. I have no clue where I'm driving. I get on the highway and speed myself up to a relaxing eighty-five miles per hour. Faster. Ninety. Who cares? Maybe life would be better if I crashed or got a speeding ticket, was pulled over, taken to jail, something.

Nah. I slow down. Sixty-five is a good speed. Yeah, well, it's the speed limit so it better be a good speed.

I don't want to get in trouble. I don't want Ashley to worry over me or think it's her fault. It's not her fault, obviously. It's mine. I'm trouble. I've always been trouble. She really needs to stay the fuck away from me.

That's going to be easier said than done. I don't know if I can stay away from her.

I need to, though.

A highway sign marks the first exit to the beach. Holy fuck, how long have I been driving? At least an hour or so. Could have come here with her. Why didn't I think of that before? Who the fuck knows! If I hadn't been such a prick to her at breakfast, I could have asked if she wanted to come to the beach. Sure, we might see someone we know there, but we could still hang out. I could watch her swim in the water in some sexy as fuck bikini.

I don't want to watch her swim in a sexy as fuck bikini. I want to strip down and get naked and go for a dip in the pool again like we did yesterday. I want to drag her to the hot tub and sit down and pull her into my lap and watch her sink onto my cock, burying it inside her pussy.

Gold. She is gold. Nah, better. Diamonds? Platinum? Tungsten? I don't know. She might as well be a fucking shooting star. I know what I am. A black hole. I ruin anything that comes close to me.

Maybe that's not very scientific. Ask Ashley about that shit. I don't know. She's not even in school for physics or science or whatever the fuck, but I bet she knows something about it anyways.

I take the exit to the beach and head towards the boardwalk. Yeah, I've done this before. Usually with friends. This isn't my first rodeo. I know how shit works around here. For good measure, I pull off my shirt at the next red light and toss it in the back. Windows down, music up, driving slow just like everyone else.

This is good. This is a good place for me. There's a lot of people here. It's nice out, so it makes sense. Girls everywhere, just walking down the side of the street near the beach. Bikinis, sarongs, the whole nine yards. Legs and ass and breasts as far as the eye can see.

I should have taken the convertible. You know how easy it is to pick up chicks in a convertible at the beach? Easier than reaching down and grabbing a handful of sand. I'll still be fine in this car, but I need a distraction and there's plenty here, so I want to make this easy.

Yeah, that's it. That's what I'll do. Drive slow. Check some girls out. Find one. Take her for a ride. More than one ride if you know what I mean. We'll see how this goes. The main beach is pretty packed, but there's some great private beaches a few miles away that aren't as crowded.

This one girl and her friend turn my way. I pretend to ignore them for a second. That's part of the charm. I want them to think they're special. I look over, see them smiling at me. I grin, wink. They giggle. One of them waves, and the other giggles even more at that, pulling her friend's hand down to stop her. I pull up alongside them.

"Hey," I say. "What's up?"

This is going to be easy. A threesome is probably exactly what I need. Who needs one girl, my stepsister, when I can have these two fine females right here and now?

Yeah, I don't know if that's a good trade off, either. I think I'm getting the short end of the stick. Whatever. I'll get over it.

2 - Ashley

Y MOM AND I GO SHOPPING, and it's alright. I
like shopping, especially with her, but it's
hard. I don't actually need any clothes. I'm
not the kind of girl that just buys a ton of clothes
whether she needs them or not, but I try to right
now. I know we can afford them now, but we
weren't always able to.

"Do you ever feel weird?" I ask her.

"What do you mean?" she asks.

"I don't know. I mean... do you ever feel weird
about all of this? With Ethan and his dad? And..."

I hold up a light summer dress that costs more
than I ever could have imagined spending on
clothes four years ago. After my mom married
Ethan's dad everything changed, though. We used
to get by, and it wasn't like we were poor or

anything, but they're rich, and so I guess now we're rich.

I just don't feel rich. I feel like I've always felt, but now I can buy hundred dollar dresses without batting an eyelash at the price tag. I still wince whenever I look at the prices, and I'm reluctant to spend that much, but... I still do it, too. It's kind of fun, like a strange guilty pleasure.

Ethan's father makes more than enough that he probably wouldn't care if I wore brand new clothes every day of the year for two decades. I wouldn't do that, though. I'd feel bad about it. I don't know why.

"Honey, we need to get used to sharing our lives with them, just like they share their lives with us. I know that you and Ethan have never really gotten along, but you should try, don't you think?"

"Mom, I'm pretty sure he's hated me since second grade," I say. "That's impressive, too, since I met him in second grade."

"A lot happened back then," my mom says. "I'm not sure it's entirely his fault. It never sounded like he hated you, either."

I know. I know what happened back then. I didn't know at the time, but I found out later.

That's when Ethan's mom died. He was out of school for awhile, but when he came back he was an entirely different person. That's saying something since we were both, what, seven or eight? It seems like such a long time ago now, and it kind of is. I've never talked about that with him. Not exactly.

I wish I knew how he felt. I wish I could say I knew what he went through. I don't, though. I'll never really know. My father left my mom when I was too young to remember. He died later, too, but I never really knew him. It was like being told you should be sad about something, but you can't really understand how or why. It's complicated. Ethan's dad's been the only man I've ever known as a father, and even then he's only been my stepfather for a few years now. It's not exactly the same.

"Does he ever say anything about me?" I ask. "Do you know if he does?"

"Who?" my mom asks.

"Ethan?"

"Oh, he mentions you sometimes," she says. "In passing."

I don't know what that means. What does that mean? "How?" I ask.

"He asks his father, who then asks me, but it's mostly just about grades. If you're doing well. Things like that. They don't talk a whole lot, but I know he's asked about you at least a couple times."

Oh. I'm not sure if she's telling me the truth. It doesn't seem right for some reason, like she's glossing over something or trying to hide something. It feels like the sort of thing someone says when they want you to think that someone cares about your well-being when they actually don't.

It's like when I used to ask my mom about my dad. My real dad. And she would say that he definitely loves me, but he just couldn't handle some things. How could she know he loves me, then? It's just something someone says. For all I know, he did love me, or he could hate me, too. I don't actually know, and I guess it doesn't even matter, either.

It's just kind of something I want to know sometimes.

How does Ethan feel about me? Does he like me, or does he hate me? Does he... love me?

No, probably not. I know this, and I know that a lot of girls wish he would fall in love with them, but it's never happened, and I don't know if it will ever happen. That's just the kind of person Ethan is. I can't change him.

I try on some dresses at my mom's urging. They're cute. We make a pile of clothes we're going to get. She mentions Jake, and asks me if I'm alright. I completely forgot about Jake. I...

"I think I'm fine," I say. "I don't want to talk about him."

"That's alright, honey," my mom says. "If you ever want to talk, I'm here for you, though. You know that, right?"

"Yeah, I know," I say. And then, mumbling, I add, "Um... since we're buying new clothes, do you think I could get some underwear, too?"

"Ooh, yes!" she says. "That's the best way to get over a break up, too. Buy something extra sexy for the next boy. That's what I always used to do."

"Mom!" I say, laughing.

She grins at me. "Ashley, it's about time you learned all there is to know about men. They're very simple. A cute pair of panties will get them every time. It's a fact."

"I'm not just going to go around showing guys my panties!" I say. "I have a little bit of self respect, you know?"

"I know," she says. "You have a lot of self respect, Ashley. And that's fine. But when it comes down to it, when you're ready to start a relationship with someone, a cute pair of panties always helps."

I roll my eyes at her. "Maybe," I say.

I wonder if Ethan likes cute panties? Well, obviously he would, right? It's not like I'm just going to randomly show him mine, but if he accidentally sees them...

No. It's over, Ashley. I have to remind myself of that. We had a nice time together. It was a really nice time, too. Now it's over, though. Done. Forever.

There's nothing either of us can do about that. It's just the way life is.

Life... it sucks sometimes! It really does.

Mia Clark

3 - Ethan

'M HOME. It's almost night time. The sun'll be setting soon. I pull into the garage and park the car, then turn it off and sit there.

Yeah, I have to go back inside, don't I? Fuck.

She's home. All the cars are here. Where else would she be? Maybe she took a walk? Maybe she's upstairs in her room, or in the living room watching TV, and I can sneak back in, go to my room, shut the door, and stay there.

Except for dinner. I can probably get out of one dinner, but then there's breakfast tomorrow. Lunch. Another dinner. There's an entire fucking summer's worth of meals and I can't skip every single one. I can't stay in my room for two months, and I can't stay out of the house for two months, either.

Basically, I'm fucked. I'm going to see Ashley one way or another, whether I want to or not, and I'm pretty much completely fucked.

Yeah, well, what can you do? I have no fucking clue. Let me know if you figure it out.

I get out of the car and head inside. My dad's hovering by the door. That's what he does when he's waiting for me to come back. He has something to say to me. I don't want to play this game, but I guess I have to. I don't even try to avoid him and get right to it.

"Hey," I say. "What's up?"

"You alright?" he asks. "I tried calling your cellphone."

I reach for my pocket to check, and... "Shit, I forgot it upstairs. Sorry."

"Wow," he says, grinning. "You forgot your phone? I didn't think anyone could live without their phones nowadays."

I grin, too, because it's kind of true. "Yeah. I had a lot on my mind. I guess I didn't notice."

"I'm sorry about earlier," my dad says. "It's been a few years, but I know you're still getting used to all of this. I am, too."

"It's cool," I say.

"I was thinking," he says, "if you're up for it, why don't we go camping soon. I can't this week, but how about next week? We can head out for a week or two. Three? Play it by ear. Like we used to, you know?"

"I'm not sure Ashley and her mom are the camping types," I say. "It's a cool idea otherwise, though."

"I meant just us," my dad says, smiling. "You and me. They can handle things here, right? We could have fun out there on our own. Be real wilderness men."

"You're just going to bring your laptop and an inflatable mattress, aren't you?" I ask, chuckling. "Not sure if that counts as being wilderness men, Dad."

"Nah," he says. "We can do it the real way. Just us, hiking in the woods. Up a mountain? Whatever you want. We don't even have to stay at a regular campground. We can take a journey through the woods and see how it goes."

It sounds fun. It sounds like something we would have done years ago. Years and years ago, before he put all of himself into his work. I know why he did it, but it's still hard to forgive him sometimes.

I'm also not sure it's something I want to do now, either. For some fucked up reason, I kind of think it'd be fun to bring Ashley and her mom camping with us. I get it. I get that this is stupid as fuck, especially considering the circumstances, but whatever. I don't care.

"I don't know," I tell him. "It sounds fun, but..." Yeah, how the fuck am I supposed to explain this to him? "I think it'd be cool to ask Ashley and her mom to come, too. I know you thought it'd be nice to go with just us, but maybe I should try to get along with them more."

Yeah, maybe I should try to stop fantasizing about burying my cock in my stepsister's pussy, too. Not sure that's ever going to happen. Not sure if I can ever just...

Just be friends with her? Fuck. Life is difficult. It really fucking sucks sometimes.

My dad lifts his brow, curious and confused. Yeah, I get it. He has a right to be.

"I think I was a dick earlier," I tell him. "I still don't want to study with her, but maybe we can hang out. I know you want me to do good in school, but I'm not her, you know? I don't know how to fucking... get good grades. I don't even understand how she does it."

My dad shrugs. "You could start by swearing less," he says with a grin.

"Yeah, shit. Sorry," I say. I don't realize until afterwards that I just swore again.

My dad laughs. "Ethan, don't ever feel like you have to be like Ashley. She's your sister now, but I hope you don't think that means you have to compete with her for anything. You're both different people, and unfortunately sometimes that means your personalities are going to clash. It also means that sometimes you can show each other something that the other would never have experienced otherwise. There's a good side and a bad side to everything."

I don't know what the good side to this is. I can see exactly what the bad side is, though.

That's me. I'm the bad boy. She's the good girl. My dad's right about that, at least.

What do bad boys do? They fuck everything up. They get into trouble. They do things they know they're not supposed to do...

They...

Holy fucking shit. I've had an epiphany. Yeah, that's right. I'm a genius. Or an idiot. One of those. I don't fucking know. I feel like I've figured some-thing important out, though. Maybe it's dumb. Yeah, it's probably dumb. It's cool, though. I feel better already.

"I think you're right," I tell my dad. "I should go apologize to her, huh?"

"It'd be nice," he says. "She's upstairs. Her and her mom went shopping, but they just came back. We're making dinner right now. It'll be ready in about thirty minutes. You want to let Ashley know? I'll call you when it's ready."

"Yeah, sounds good," I say.

My dad puts a hand on my shoulder, strong and steady. We're not good at this. We don't deal with emotions well. There's too many of them. That shit's confusing as fuck. Oh well, who cares?

I hug him. Whatever. He hugs me, too. It's real fucking manly.

We let go of each other and he heads back to the kitchen with Ashley's mom. I've got a date with destiny or some shit like that. I've remembered something important just now, and I've got to deal with it. This can't wait.

I go upstairs, kick off my shoes in my room, and my socks, too, then head to Ashley's room. Her door is open. I walk right in, don't even knock, don't even say anything. She's standing with her back to me, poking through a bag of clothes she must have just bought today. Didn't she just buy new clothes the other day with that friend of hers? Julia or whatever?

Now she's got more. And... huh. She's holding up a pair of cute as fuck panties, twirling them this way and that in her hands, stretching them out and looking at them from every angle. Shit, I'd love to see those on her. They're lacy and light blue, boy short styled, and I'm pretty sure her ass would look amazing in them.

I close the door behind me, not even trying to hide the fact that I'm there anymore. She jumps, startled, and turns towards me. I grin at her, then click the lock on her door, trapping us in her room.

"What are you doing?" she asks me, eyes narrowed.

"I went to the beach today," I tell her. "You know what happened when I was there?"

"Um... no..."

"I was driving around," I say. "I was pissed off. I wanted to do something stupid. I saw these two girls, and they were looking at me. Real DTF, giggling and shit."

"DTF?" she asks.

"Down to fuck," I say.

"Ethan," she says. "Please, stop. I don't want to hear this. I don't want to hear about your... your conquests, or whatever you want to call them."

"Listen," I say. "First off, fuck you, Princess. You know why? Because nothing happened. I was going to. I was going to screw shit up bad and make you hate me, because I wanted to forget everything and it's probably better if you really fucking hate me. I didn't, though. I said hi to them and then I kept driving. That's all I've done all day is drive. That's it."

"I don't know why you're telling me this," she says.

"There's a reason," I say. "I'm telling you this because even though shit's kind of fucked up right now, we had rules, and I wanted to stick to them. Rule number... whatever the hell it was. What rule are we dealing with here?"

She knows. I know she knows.

"Rule number ten," she whispers to me. "You can't sleep with other girls while we're..." She pauses. "But we're not now. I don't know what you're trying to say."

"We're not?" I ask her. "You sure about that, Princess? I think you're forgetting the most important fucking rule, don't you?"

She scrunches up her nose and looks at me, trying to figure out what I mean.

"Rule number one," I tell her. "This is only going to last a week. Guess what? The week isn't over yet. Not by a fucking longshot, Princess. I didn't realize it until I got home, but that's what's been screwing with me this entire time. I almost forgot the rules, but I'm glad I remembered."

"A week!" she says, glaring at me. "It was a week because that's how long our parents were going to be away. I think it's kind of over now, Ethan. They're back already."

"Fuck you," I say. "Yeah, for real, just fuck you, Princess. A week is a fucking week. If you want to stop, then you're going to have to use rule number three. I remember that one, at least."

"I can change my mind whenever I want," she says.

"Yeah," I say. "You can. Do it. I dare you. I'll leave right now if you do. We can end this on our own terms, Princess. It's your decision."

"I don't think it's that easy," she says. "Ethan, I..."

"Fucking do it!" I growl at her. "Say it's over! Tell me you're done and you don't want to do this anymore."

Her bottom lip trembles and she starts to shake. It hurts to watch her. I don't want to yell at her like this, but I just need to make her understand. I think that's what we're both missing here. Closure. She can end it. If she wants to end it, she can end it. And then it's done. That's our choice. It's not done because we have to stop because our parents came home. It's done because she wants it to be done. That's the rule. It's our rule.

"What if I don't want to say it?" she asks, whispering, nervous.

"You remember what rule number two is?" I ask her

She smiles softly and nods.

"Come here, Princess. Right fucking now. Get the hell over here."

Mia Clark

4 - *Ashley*

I DON'T KNOW WHAT'S WRONG WITH HIM. In addition to that, I don't know what's wrong with me. Why am I even considering doing this? Our parents are right downstairs! They could hear us. They could come up looking for us. They could stand right outside our door and knock and ask to come in, and then what?

I can say no, I guess. I can be quiet, too. I don't know if I want to be quiet, though. Maybe they won't come up at all?

I hesitate, and Ethan stares at me.

I stare back at him. Hard. This is my room, isn't it? He's not the boss here, I am, and...

I don't know. That's as far as I get with that line of thinking. I have another thought, though, and I kind of like it.

"What if I don't want to?" I ask him, haughty, smirking.

"Oh, you're going to play that game?" he asks. "You want to, Princess. Don't deny it."

I shake my head and lift my chin up. "Nope!"

"You're making me so much fucking harder right now," he says. "I'm going to make you pay for that."

He steps towards me, but I'm quick. I think I'm quick, at least. I leap over my bed, scattering my clothes from the shopping bag, and dive for the other side to slip away from him.

It doesn't go very well. Ethan grabs my ankles and stops my dive, then pulls me back slightly. He moves his hands up my legs towards my thighs, then flips me around onto my back. I'm trapped now, pinned on the bed by his strong arms while he looms over me with an intense look in his eyes.

"Now why'd you have to do that?" he asks, smirking.

I cross my arms over my chest and pretend not to look at him, even though I can see him out of the corner of my eye. "Because," I say.

"Because what?" he asks. "Because of this morning?"

"You were kind of mean, huh?" I ask. "Actually, yes and no. I was really upset about that, Ethan."

He lets go of my legs and slides onto the bed next to me. I turn to face him and we lay like that, sideways across the bed, both of us staring into the other's eyes.

"Yeah," he says. "Look, I'm sorry about that, Ashley. Can you forgive me?"

"Why'd you do it?" I ask him. I'm curious to know the answer, but I"m even more curious to hear him apologize and ask for forgiveness. I don't think I've ever heard Ethan Colton do something like that on his own before.

"I was angry," he says. He refuses to elaborate.

"If you want me to forgive you, you have to talk to me, alright?" I tell him. "You need to tell me everything."

"I don't do this," he says. "It's too much like... like shit I don't do."

I understand. It's too much like a relationship, which is something we can't have. But maybe we can, too? I don't know.

"Ethan," I say, reaching out to touch his cheek. "I know what we're doing is um... unorthodox? I want you to know that no matter what happens, you're like my family now, too, though. Your dad is my stepdad and my mom is your stepmom, and we're stepsiblings, so I think we should be able to talk to each other about things."

He looks away for a second, but then he turns back to me. There's some look in his eyes that startles me for a second. It's different from how he usually looks at things; how he usually looks at me.

"I'm not used to talking about emotional bullshit," he says. "It's easier to just move on and forget it."

"Is that what you want to do then?" I ask. "You want to move on and forget this?"

"No," he says. "That's the problem. I like what was going on. I'm pissed that our parents came back early and they're ruining it. You want to know what I thought about while I was driving?" he asks.

"What?"

"Stupid shit," he says with a grin. "Just dumb, stupid shit. I was thinking about how we could get a hotel room or something for the rest of the week and do our own thing there. Maybe go on a vacation or something. Hang out in Cancun or Aruba or wherever the fuck, I don't know. Then we wouldn't have to stop early and we could have a good time."

"You weren't really thinking that, were you?" I ask him. I don't know how he could. He just... he confuses me. He seemed so upset this morning. So dismissive of everything involving me, that I'm not sure how he could have thought of any of that.

"Yeah, I don't know," he says, shrugging slightly. "It's fucked up."

"I really like you," I say without thinking. Oh God, did I just say that? "Um... as a friend, I mean. Stepbrother. With benefits. Or without benefits. I think. This is the first time we've ever really talked a lot, huh?"

"Yeah," he says. "I guess so. You're pretty cool, yourself. I don't hate you."

"Oh, you don't hate me?" I say, rolling my eyes at him. "Thanks a lot!"

"I like you, Princess. I'd hang out with you, even if we weren't going to fuck."

"Me, too," I say, nodding quick. "But, we are. As soon as you get my pants off."

"Shit, is that a challenge?" he asks.

"Um... yes, maybe, because we have to be quiet!" I say. "Maybe this won't work. I don't know how this is going to work. Do you really think we're going to be able to sneak this past our parents for the rest of the week?"

"I've got an idea," he says, smirking. "What I'm really curious about is how we're going to manage rule number fifteen."

"That's the..." It takes me a moment, but then I remember. "That's impossible! We definitely can't do that one."

"Nah, your rule, Princess. I didn't make it. You can't give up now."

"They'll figure it out," I say. "Ethan, we can't sleep in the same room together. It's not going to work."

"We're sleeping in the same room together," he says. "Tonight you're going to come to my room. You think I'm just going to give up on this? You're wrong."

He says all of this while sitting up and reaching towards my pants. His fingers unbutton my jeans and tug on the waistband, pulling them down my hips. Then a little lower, lower still, until he has them all the way off. He tosses them on the floor by the side of the bed.

"Maybe we can... I can sneak out," I say. I'm distracted. I don't realize he's pulling at the waistband of my panties at first.

"Hey, some help here?" he asks. "Lift that beautiful fucking ass of yours up so I can pull this shit off and shove my cock in your glorious pussy."

"Wow, really? You're so romantic. Do you seriously say these things to girls? I don't know how you ever have sex."

"Please?" he asks, grinning. "I want to taste your sweet pussy first, too. You're fucking delicious, Princess."

Well, I can't really object to that, now can I? Because I do kind of want him to lick me there. Um... it was very good last time, and...

Our parents are seriously right downstairs! We definitely shouldn't be doing this. Unfortunately my hips are intent on giving in to Ethan's seductions, and they seemingly lift of their own accord. He pulls my panties slowly down my legs and I lay there on the bed, bare from the waist down.

"Fuck, you're beautiful," he says, staring at my crotch.

"Not really," I say to him. "You just like my pussy."

"Nah," he says. He claps a hand against my sex, holding me there tight, and then he moves up until his face is right over mine, our lips almost touching. "I don't usually say this shit, Princess, but since you're my stepsister, I'll make an exception. You're beautiful everywhere. You're pretty as fuck, cute, and a lot of fun. Not just sex fun, either. You're the entire fucking package."

I don't know what to say to that. I reach up and cup his cheeks with my hands and then pull him down to kiss him. He comes and he kisses me while his hand holds my bare pussy. He slides his fingers up and down, teasing at my arousal.

I have something to admit. I know this is strange, but I've been horny all day. I've missed being able to see and touch and feel Ethan whenever I want, and I thought about maybe masturbating, but um... mostly I was with my mom, so that wouldn't really work, you know? When we finally came home and I went upstairs to look at my clothes and put them away, I was seriously considering locking my door, laying down on my bed and...

But now I don't have to. Ethan is here. He can do it for me? The thought makes me giggle into his kiss, and he pulls back, giving me a funny look.

"Something funny?" he asks.

"Yes," I say. "Why are you taking so long to have sex with me? I'm ready, if you haven't noticed."

"Holy fuck, being sassed by a chick with no pants. This is unreal. You want my cock that bad, Princess?"

I bite my bottom lip and nod at him. "I would not be opposed to it," I say.

"Yeah yeah, hold the fuck on..." He gets up, pulling away from me.

My body misses the heat of his hand as soon as he's gone. I feel the chill of the open air caressing against my slick arousal. To make up for his loss, I sneak my hand between my legs and start playing with myself. Ethan undoes his pants, slow at first, but when he sees me touching between my legs, he hurries up fast.

Now he's naked from the waist down like me. Pants on the floor, shoes kicked off, no socks, underwear gone... His cock throbs and bounces in front of me. I lick my lips, staring at him. I think this is going to be a lot of fun...

"I wanted to do this properly," he says. "We don't have a lot of time, though. Dinner's going to be ready soon. Probably ten or fifteen minutes now. So, yeah, this is going to be quick as fuck, Princess. I'll make it up to you later. Promise."

I start to answer him, to say that's fine, that I just want him right now, that I need him, but he stifles me by pressing his lips hard against mine.

His mouth, those lips, against um... not my mouth... not those lips...

He slaps my hand away from my pussy and grabs my thighs, then pulls me across the bed closer to him. Lifting me up until only my shoulders and my head are the only things touching the bed, he pulls my thighs over his shoulders and buries his mouth into my wet, bare pussy. The sensation is instant, almost shocking, like falling through the ice while walking across a frozen lake in the winter. This is a good shock, though.

My body bucks and writhes as his tongue laps at my slit. He tickles the tip of his tongue against my clit, side to side, then up and around, slow, fast, everything. His hands hold me up, fingers digging into my butt, keeping me pressed tight against his mouth.

"Oh my God!" I scream out. When I realize what's going on, I clap my hand over my mouth, trying to quiet myself down. This is a huge struggle, though. This is exciting in all the wrong ways. I really shouldn't be excited at my step-brother um... eating me out... when our parents are right downstairs. For some reason that makes it kind of more exciting, though. This is so wrong it's ridiculous, and the risk makes it all the more interesting.

My stomach flutters, a mix of nervous butter-flies and orgasmic anticipation. Because, mhm, I'm pretty sure that's where we're going with this.

Ethan lays me back on the bed softly. His lips are wet and glistening from my arousal. "Holy fuck, Princess," he says. "I could eat you out all day."

"Maybe tomorrow?" I offer.

"Don't even fucking tempt me," he says. "I'll drag you to a fucking airport, get us both tickets on the next flight to who gives a fuck, and do what-ever the hell I want with you for days."

"Really!" I say, laughing. "It sounds fun, but maybe a little more romance?"

"What do you want from me here? Cover the bed in roses and then drench your pussy in red wine while I eat you out?"

"Um... actually that would be kind of hot," I say, squirming.

"Oh yeah?" he asks. He slides my butt on the bed, moving my head closer to my pillows.

I nod quick. "Mhm."

"I don't usually do shit like that, but I'd do it for you," he says.

It's just so... so crass, but romantic, too? But in a weird way, because I don't think this is supposed to be romantic. We aren't romancing each other, we're just doing a stepbrother with benefits thing.

Right? Yes... I think so... I'm not sure anymore.

Now is not the time to think about that, though.

"Here's how we'll do this," he says. "You need to be quiet, right? Me too. So first we--" He grabs my hips and before I realize it I'm flipped over onto my stomach. "--just like that, and then if you have to scream or anything, bury your face in a pillow. Got it?"

"Very scientific and technical," I say, laughing.

"Don't fucking sass me, Princess," he says.

Ethan laughs, too. Not for the same reasons at all. He laughs because in the middle of telling me not to sass him, he lines his cock up with the entrance to my pussy and thrusts all the way into me. When he finishes his sentence, I let out a sharp

gasp, arching my back. Thankfully my face natural-
ly ends up in a pillow, because right after thrusts
inside of me I make a lot of noises. I'm not even
sure what I'm saying, but it's loud and uncontrol-
lable.

Ethan grabs my hips and pulls me up slightly,
bringing the center of my body a little ways off the
bed. He sneaks his hand towards my stomach, then
down to my clit, and starts rubbing lightly. When
he's set himself up nicely, he pulls out of me, then
thrusts hard back in. His other hand holds my hip,
keeping me in place and pulling my body harder
onto his cock.

I reach for a pillow. Another pillow. I grab it. I
shove it under my face and scream as loud as I can
into it. It's kind of fun and cathartic in a weird way.
I can hear myself, but I hope no one else can.

I didn't know I was this worked up. Before
being with Ethan, I didn't know I could even be
this worked up. I'd only had orgasms with myself,
never with someone else, and the sex I had was
um... not very exciting. It felt nice, and I thought
that's what sex was. It was just something nice.

No. Apparently not. Sex with Ethan is raw and
primal and hard. It isn't *nice*, it's reality-shattering.
With each of his thrusts, I can feel my entire world
falling to pieces all around me. There's so much
sensation existing inside me, there's so many
wonderful feelings to experience, and I never even
knew any of this existed before.

I cum. I was more than ready to, and I do. Usually it takes me a little longer when we're further into having sex, but not now. Ethan keeps teasing and toying with my clit while he thrusts hard into me, but I can tell it's a little more difficult for him with me squeezing and clutching against him.

"Fuck, did you just cum?" he asks. He sounds cocky and overly arrogant, but I guess he has a reason for it right now.

I shift my mouth away from the pillow, turning my head to the side. "Shut up and keep going," I say.

He laughs, but quietly, a little bit. "I wasn't planning on stopping," he says. "Not yet."

Something comes over me. This is too insane. I don't know why I'm doing this, or what we're even doing. This is not something that girls like me do. Ethan's corrupted me, hasn't he? Except I kind of like being corrupted. I guess a corrupted person *would* say that, wouldn't they?

It's just...

One orgasm leads into the next. I'm not sure the first ever stopped. I didn't know I could have multiple orgasms before now, but here I am, having them. It's another new experience, and it's absolutely amazing. My body shivers and thrives on its newfound sexual energy.

To make up for my clenching resistance, Ethan shifts up, right above me now. He pushes his hand on the small of my back, holding me down, then slams hard into me. My body resists him because of my climax, but at this vantage point it doesn't matter. He is filling me whether the inner depths of my pussy want him to or not.

I don't care what *they* want. *I* want him to fill me.

My body cools. Not completely, but my last orgasm trembles away to a more steady, even moment of passion. I think it does, at least. My arousal flares up again when Ethan spanks my ass hard and sends a smacking echo through my room. I clench my eyes shut and moan into the pillow again, trying to stifle the noise.

He does it again. My body quivers beneath him. My ass shakes. He thrusts hard into me and smacks my butt and...

Oh my God it's loud, isn't it? I turn to say something to him, but it just comes out in a garbled mess of partial nonsense words.

"You want me to be quieter? Then cum again for me, Princess," he says. He must have understood me whether I thought I made sense or not.

I didn't think I liked being spanked before this. I'm not even sure if I do like being spanked or not, or if it's more to do with the fact that all of this is wrong. Having sex with Ethan is wrong, doing it in my bed when our parents are downstairs is wrong, and now him spanking me makes it even more wrong, and...

I give in to him. Again. He's tiring, getting tired. How long have we been having sex? I glance over at the clock on my bedside table, and it hasn't even been that long. How is this possible? It's like time is standing still all around us while we condense these intense sexual sensations into a fraction of the amount of time they should take.

We've discovered it. We've discovered the secret to time travel, haven't we?

It all comes crashing back, though. Time speeds up again and my body convulses in another orgasm. I belatedly realized this isn't my third, it's my fourth. I don't know how that happened. I'm really not sure. I can't explain it.

Ethan presses hard into me with one final thrust and grabs my hips with both of his hands, pulling himself as far into me as he can. His cock twitches and throbs. I know what's coming next, but my own body is betraying me in treacherous orgasm already. He cums, filling me as deeply as he can, while my inner walls grab and milk his cock, begging him for more.

This is so... it's so perfect. How can something so wrong be so perfect at the same time?

I don't know. I don't think I want to ever know. I just want to live in the moment, to be where I am right now, and not think about anything else.

I want to stay here. Forever. I want to be with him...

That's not a part of this. It won't work. I know we can't. I still kind of wish we could.

Ethan slips out of me and slaps my butt one last time.

"Let's go, Princess," he says. "Mom and Dad are waiting."

Cool, cocky, and confident. He gets up off my bed like we didn't just fuck with wild, reckless abandon. It was wild. And reckless. It was amazing, too, though.

"I can't believe we did that," I say, in awe and disbelief.

"You know you loved it," he says. Bending down, he grabs his pants off my bedroom floor.

I lay on the bed, feeling the remnants of him inside me. I like it. It feels right for some reason. I watch him pulling his pants on. They hang loose on his hips even after he's zipped and buttoned them. I like the way his abs tense when he moves, even small movements, and I like how there's a little muscular V near his hips, like there's an arrow pointing the way to his sexual treasure.

A sign to lead me, or one to warn me away from danger. I still haven't figured out which it is yet. I'm still half naked long after he finishes putting his clothes on and fixing himself up to look mostly regular again. He gives me a look. It's a strange look. I don't know what it means at first, but then...

He's on me. Above me. Two of his fingers thrust deep inside me, claiming my sex as his. I gasp and arch my back, eyes rolling into my head.

"Ethan!" I gasp.

"Listen, Ashley, you think you can get away with looking at me like that, laying on your bed with no pants on?" he asks. "Nah, I don't think so. You're still mine right now. Yeah, that's a good girl." He moves his fingers inside of me and I writhe and squirm at his touch. "Fuck, you're so sensitive. How many orgasms did you have? Tell me."

I whimper and moan, but he ignores me.

"Tell me. Now. How many?"

"Four," I whisper.

"Louder."

"Mom and Dad will... they'll hear us, Ethan," I tell him. If they haven't heard us already, that is. "You need to stop."

"You think I care?" he growls. "Tell me how many orgasms you had? Your pussy is mine, and I want to keep track."

"Four," I say again. I realize immediately this is a lie, though. My body is betraying me again, and small tremors of ecstatic excitement shiver through me. There's something wrong with me, isn't there? I shouldn't get this excited, especially now. We really do need to stop.

I admit it, though. Judging by the grin on his face, he already knows. "Five," I say, blushing.

He thrusts his fingers into me harder now, sending me into thrashing spasms on the bed. I hold my hands over my mouth to keep from screaming out my lust. Finally he stops, and I stop, but we're not done yet.

He brings his fingers to my mouth, the same ones that were just inside me. "Taste," he says.

My God, this... this is wrong. All of this is wrong, though. I'm getting too attached to this. I'm becoming too wrapped up in it. I wish it wasn't happening. Not because I want it to stop. I wish Ethan wasn't my stepbrother. I wish we could...

We can't.

I open my mouth without thinking and lick and suck at his fingers like they're his cock. I glance towards his crotch while I taste everything he has to offer me, which is everything I had to offer him, and, yes, he's erect again. He's as aroused as me. Maybe I don't have to suck his fingers? Maybe I can... do we have enough time?

He pulls his finger away and smirks at me. "Now put some damn pants on," he says. "Mom and Dad are waiting for us."

No sooner than he says it, I hear something, though. I'm not sure how we didn't hear this before. Footsteps, coming down the hall. Closer. Right outside my door. Panicking, I glance towards the door, but it's locked. Ethan locked it before he came in.

"Fuck," he says, hushed.

Well yeah! Fuck is right!

Someone knocks softly, and a second later I hear Ethan's dad. "Ashley, is everything alright? I thought I heard something."

I freeze. Ethan glares at me, then nudges my shoulder a little. Oh, right! Um...

"Tell him it's alright, Princess," he whispers. "You're up. This is your time to shine."

The way he says it almost makes me laugh, but I stop myself because this really isn't funny! This is honestly more than a little scary. My heart races and I breathe in deep, then exhale, trying to calm myself down.

"Yes, um... sorry. I was in the shower."

"It's alright," my stepdad says. "I just wanted to let you know that dinner's ready."

"Alright!" I say. Too excited. Calm down! He's going to suspect something. "I'll be down in a second. Sorry."

"No rush. Me and your mom just finished up. Have you seen Ethan? Did he come to talk to you?"

I glance over at Ethan. Have I seen him? Um, yes, he's standing here right now. Also, I still don't have pants on. I stand up, legs shaking, and go to get them.

I start putting them on and say, "Um... yes, he did. He... well, I haven't seen him since then. I don't know where he is. He's not here now. Because I was just in the shower, of course. So he wouldn't be. That would just be weird."

Ethan gives me the most deadpan look I've ever seen. He doesn't say anything, but he doesn't

40

have to. Are you serious, Princess? Are you seriously serious? Did you just say all of that? That's what he says to me with his eyes.

I glare back at him and shake my head, eyes wide, lips curled, tongue sticking out. What was I supposed to say!

"Alright," Ethan's dad says. "I hope you two are doing better. I know it's rough sometimes. I checked his room, but he isn't there. If you see him, could you tell him dinner's ready? Maybe he slipped outside. I'll go check."

"Sure," I say. "I will."

Ethan's dad starts to walk away. I hear him stop a few steps down the hall, though. I freeze. Again. Ethan freezes, too. Sort of. He doesn't look nearly as frozen as me.

A couple of seconds later, his dad keeps going, heading to the stairs.

"Apparently you're outside," I say, glancing towards the window. "Maybe you should jump out so your dad doesn't suspect anything?"

"Did you seriously just tell me to go jump out a window?" he asks.

"I don't know!"

"You don't know if you told me to jump out a window? I can tell you for sure that you did," he says, grinning.

"I was just saying," I say.

"How are you going to explain going down to dinner without wet hair after you apparently just took a shower?" Ethan asks.

"Oh no... wait, I just didn't wash my hair. That's it. Today isn't the day I wash my hair. It'll work. It makes sense."

"Or you could take a shower," he says.

"I don't have time to take a shower, Ethan! Dinner's ready. Didn't you hear your dad?"

"Yeah, so you're going to go down like that, Princess?" he asks. "You realize I just filled you up. Came inside you. Your pussy is coated. For real. You sure you don't want to sneak in a quick shower?"

"Why did you have to say that?" I ask. "Why did you have to remind me?"

"Just go downstairs like that," he says, grinning. "No big deal. Eat dinner in front of your mom and my dad with my cum leaking out of you. What do I care?"

"Gross. Ick."

"How about this," he says. "Later, after dinner, when we're both going to bed, I'll take a shower with you. I'll clean you inside and out, Princess. What do you say?"

He moves close to me, grabbing my chin in his hand, lifting it up so that my eyes meet his.

"You're just trying to trick me," I tell him, rolling my eyes. "Once I'm clean, you're just going to make me dirty again, aren't you?"

"You want me to? You want to be my dirty girl, Princess?"

I don't answer. I don't answer because, yes, I kind of do? A little bit? Maybe a lot. I don't know how we're going to do this. It's not going to work. Someone's going to find out. Someone is going to catch us, and then what?

It's only for a week, though. That's it. We can do it. I can do this! I think. I hope. I really want to.

I like how Ethan makes me feel. It's not just my body, but it's everything. I like how we can laugh, even during sex. I thought sex was supposed to be serious before, but Ethan makes it fun. I like how we can cuddle after, even without sex. I like how I'm going to sleep in his room tonight. I don't know how that's going to work. I don't think I can explain that to my mom if she finds us in there together, cuddled under the blankets on his bed, but...

I just want to do it anyways. I like how he's warm and rough and hard and soft and gentle and careful but he pushes my limits, too. I like how wrong this is, but how right it feels, and it hurt before. It hurt when he left me like that, it hurt when he said things like that at breakfast, but Ethan is a bad boy. I've heard him say a lot worse to other people.

He's mine, though. He's my bad boy. For a week. We don't have a lot of time left. I want to savor it.

It's all I'll ever have of him. I don't know what kind of relationship we'll have after that. I don't know if we'll have anything. I don't know if it's possible.

I try to convince myself it will be fine having Ethan as a friend, as just my stepbrother.

I try, but I'm not sure if I succeed.

I put my panties and pants back on, then we listen at the door to make sure no one's there. Sneaking out together, we head to the stairs to go down and eat dinner with our parents. Before we do, he grabs me and pushes me up against a wall and kisses me. His hands roam up my sides towards my breasts, and he gropes and fondles me like that. One hand sneaks lower, to my crotch, feeling me up in the middle of the hallway.

I don't care. I kiss him back. It's just for a second. Two, three, four. We're done. He pulls away from me, and only then do I fully realize what we just did.

I open my mouth, gaping, and just stare at him.

"Did you really just do that?" I ask.

"See you downstairs, Princess," Ethan says, grinning. "Dinner's ready. Don't forget."

5 - Ethan

DINNER WAS...

a) interesting
b) fucked up
c) difficult because I had a hard-on the entire time
d) all of the above

I'll let you decide. I don't know what was going on there. The food was good, though. Ashley's mom is a good cook, and my dad's alright. He mostly just helps her with stuff. Cooking our own meals is kind of a recent occurrence in my house. We used to do it when I was really young, but then things happened and we stopped. My dad would always order out, or have someone come over and make the food for us, whatever. After he married Ashley's mom, things changed, though.

I'm kind of glad. It's nice.

Anyways, dinner was alright. Not a lot going on. We talked. Everyone talked. I'm not big on family chit chat, but I can do it when I need to, and I felt like I owed it to Ashley, so yeah. There you go. That's what happened.

She went upstairs right after dinner, though. Took a shower. What the fuck bullshit is that? I thought we were taking a shower together. I guess I don't blame her.

And the evening progressed like that. Nothing crazy. Not yet, at least. Just hold on, give me a second.

We're downstairs now, all of us, hanging out in the living room, watching TV. I don't know why I'm there. Usually I wouldn't be, but Ashley's mom asked me to hang around. Sure, whatever, why not? It's not like I have anything else to do right now. It's not like I can tell her I'd rather sneak away to fuck her daughter. How messed up would that be?

Yeah, do you mind if me and my stepsister just go upstairs and get naked, Mom? Dad, you don't care, right? I kind of want to fuck the shit out of her, then rest for a little while and do it again. Don't worry, she'll like it. If you hear her screaming my name, it's cool. Don't wait up.

Nah, that's never going to happen. I've still got some sense of decency, no matter what you think.

Eventually the night winds down, though. Ashley says she's going to bed. I wait a few minutes. This is our plan. I have no idea why we need a plan like this, but sure, I'll go along with it.

"I think I'm going to go to bed, too," I say.

"Alright, Ethan," my stepmom says. "Thanks for spending time with us tonight. We've missed you. It's nice to have everyone back under one roof again, even if it's just for the summer."

"Yeah," I say. "It was cool. I had fun."

"Think about what I said earlier," my dad says. "Let me know soon. We can plan something."

"Oh?" Ashley's mom says. "You're both planning something?"

My dad grins and shakes his head. "Manly secrets, honey. Don't you worry about it."

I roll my eyes. My dad's kind of a dork sometimes, especially when it comes to Ashley's mom. They're cute together, though. Good couple. It's nice to see my dad happy again, I guess. It's nice to have a mom again, even though I never really thought something like that would work out.

You never know what kind of fucked up shit is going to work out until you just go with it, though. That's how life is. Stranger things have happened. Like what's happening right now with me and Ashley.

I say good night again and then head upstairs. I walk down the hall to my room, open the door, turn the lights on, and...

Holy fuck. I've got a present.

Ashley lays sprawled out on my bed, completely naked, legs spread slightly, with her hands holding her breasts and tweaking her nipples. Can't say I mind the view. In fact, it's a delicious fucking view. I close my bedroom door and lock it, then I stare at her, appreciating every fucking beautiful inch of her body.

"What if someone else came in before me?" I ask her.

"Who else would come in?" she says.

I shrug. "I don't know. Anyone. Your mom? My dad? Batman? I don't fucking know. I'm just saying it's not a good idea to get naked on a bed unless you know what you're dealing with."

"I think I know what I'm dealing with..." she says, grinning.

"You think so, do you?" Yeah, I don't think she does. She doesn't even know the half of it. The things I would do to this girl...

"Are you going to come to bed or are you just going to stand there?" she asks.

Man, she's getting way too cocky. That's supposed to be my thing. I strip down, making a show of it. She watches me from the bed. I'm naked now, hard as fuck, and I walk over to her, standing at the edge of my bed.

"Listen, Princess. I'm not in the mood to play around right now. I just want to fuck you hard. You down?"

Yeah, well, guess what? She is.

This isn't pretty. There's no romance here. I mean, yeah, it's nice. It's art, in that creative, raw, and primal realism sort of way. I seriously just want to fuck her, though. I can't stop thinking about it. It's not even just that, though. You know what comes after fucking? I'm learning about that, too. Usually what comes after is me leaving, or me politely kicking the girl out and sending her home, but not now

I slam hard into her. We're done. This is it. She's on her back, knees wrapped around my waist, hands clinging to my neck, refusing to let go. Fuck, she's tight. All of her is tight. Inside and out. She clenches around my cock while she clings to my neck and my waist and it's like her entire fucking body is orgasming around my body. I can feel her cum, and I join her.

It's a really good thing she's on birth control, because I'm pretty fucking sure her womb is about to be overflowing with my seed. The thought is kind of hot, in a fucked up way. Impregnating my stepsister? Breeding the fuck out of her? Watching her stomach bulge with my baby? Yeah, uh, no. It's kind of sexy to think about it, except I'm pretty sure if that happened, I'd end up dead. Either her mom or my dad, or maybe even Ashley herself would do it. I don't have a death wish.

I still can't stop thinking about it. Oh well.

We roll over and lay on our backs. I sweep the blankets over us, covering us, and then reach up to flick a switch to turn off the lights. It's dark, but I can hear her breathing next to me. After a few seconds, she scoots closer and lays her head on my chest, wrapping her arm around me.

"That was nice," she says.

"Nice? That's it?" I ask. "Shit, I didn't do a good enough job. Give me a second and I'll make it up to you, Princess."

She laughs. "Shush, you. Let's just cuddle."

"I don't cuddle," I say. "You realize that, don't you?"

"Please?" she says, whispering into my ear. She kisses my earlobe, then my cheek, then closer to my mouth.

"Yeah yeah," I say, grumbling. Truth is, I really want to cuddle with her, though. It's relaxing as fuck. "So how's this going to work?" I ask.

"I have my phone," she says. "It's on your bedside table. I set my alarm for earlier than usual, so I can wake up and sneak back to my room, then go back to bed or just go downstairs."

"How about you wake up, we have sex, then go back to bed, wake up, have sex again, and then you go back to your room?" I ask.

She hits my chest softly, playful. "Do you ever think about anything besides sex?" she asks, smiling.

"Yeah," I say. "Sometimes."

"Like what?" she asks. She sounds interested.

I shrug. "Lots of shit. The future, I guess. The past."

"Me too," she says. "Do you ever want to talk about it?"

"What's there to talk about?"

She shrugs this time. "Why'd you always cause so much trouble in school?"

I roll my eyes. Not this conversation. I've had it a million times with a million people. It's boring. Real old.

"Why'd you always get perfect grades in school?" I counter.

She answers me, though. I didn't expect that one. "I guess it's the only thing I feel like I'm good at," she says. "It was the only thing I could think of that I could do that would impress people, but no one was ever really impressed. After awhile, everyone just expected it, so I had to keep doing it, or else they'd think something was wrong with me."

"Yeah," I say. "Me too."

"You didn't get very good grades, though," she says.

"Wow. Thanks for stating the obvious, Little Miss Perfect. I meant that's why I did stupid shit. People just expected it. Everyone would always come to me asking me to help them with dumb junk, so I'd usually just do it. There were some other reasons, too, I guess."

"Why'd you always flip my skirt up in second grade?" she asks.

I laugh. "You don't want to know the answer to that one, Princess."

"Nope, I do," she says, adamant.

"It's not that hard to figure out," I say. "I wanted to see your underwear."

She blushes. I can't see it because it's dark, but I can feel the heat from her cheeks pressing against my chest. It's a big blush, too. I pull her closer to me and reach my arm down her back, then grab her ass. Aw yeah. She blushes even more, and squirms, too.

"We were seven," she says eventually, whispering. "Maybe eight. I don't remember now. You didn't really want to see my underwear. That's not what little boys think about."

"You wanted an answer and I told you," I say. "I wanted to see your underwear. I still want to see your underwear. What was that cute as fuck little ensemble you had earlier? Where'd you get those?"

"Did you like them?" she asks. "I bought them at the store. They aren't for you to see, Ethan. They're for someone else."

"Who the fuck else?" I ask. "I don't like the sound of this."

"I don't know. My next boyfriend, I guess."

"You should show them to me," I say.

"Are you offering to be my boyfriend?" she asks, coy as fuck.

"I think we both know that's not going to work," I say.

"Why not?" she asks.

Holy fuck, is she serious? "First off, I don't do that. Second, how the fuck do you think that's going to work?"

She shrugs. "I'm just teasing you. Calm down, Mr. Bad Boy."

"Wow. You've got some balls, Princess. I'll give you that."

She reaches between my legs for my balls, and cups them in her hand. "Mine?" she asks.

"Yeah, I'll give that to you," I say, smirking. "Balls deep in your pussy. How's that sound?"

"Mmm," she murmurs. "But I like talking to you, too."

"I don't know why," I say.

"You're interesting," she says. "I think there's a lot more to you than you want to let on, Ethan Colton."

"Nah."

"Can we really still be friends after this?" she asks. "Do you think we can or not?"

"I guess we can try," I say. I don't add that I don't think we can, because I'm just going to want to fuck her, and obviously that's not going to work.

The thing is that I want to do more than that, too, though. I want to cuddle. I want to learn more about her. I want to talk. I want to go have fun, to hang out, to get to know each other. I've never really felt this way about anyone before. Yeah, I hang out with the guys on the football team, and we talk and shit, get to know each other, but it's not really too personal. We don't talk about our dreams and aspirations. We don't talk about our hopes and goals and emotions and feelings, whatever the fuck.

"I want to," I say. "It's just hard."

"Why?" she asks.

"Because every time I look at you, I can't stop thinking about how it would feel to slam my cock into your pussy."

"Then don't look," she says. She reaches up and covers my eyes with her hand. "See? Now we can talk about anything we want to talk about."

I laugh. "Cute. Real cute, Princess."

"Do you want to get better grades?" she asks. "I can help you, you know? We could have Skype chats and be study buddies."

"Yeah, that's just what I need," I say, rolling my eyes. "A study buddy."

"If you're really good, we could do other things, too, Ethan..."

I both like and dislike the sound of that. "Yeah?"

"Mhm," she says. "Maybe I could let you see me play with myself, and maybe you could let me see you do the same, too."

"That sounds like two things that won't ever work," I say. "A long distance relationship and screwing around with my stepsister over video chat? Uh... yeah..."

"I know it's supposed to be just a week," she says. "I know that's what we said, and then we stopped because our parents came back, and um...

now we're naked in bed again. I know it's wrong, Ethan, but I don't want it to be. Do you want it to last longer? If you could, I mean. Would you want it to?"

I don't say anything. I can't encourage her with this. It doesn't matter what I want.

"I do," she says. "I know I shouldn't say that, but I want it to last longer. I wish it could. Maybe it can?"

Please don't say stuff like that. That's what I want to tell her, but I don't. I stay silent, because I'm a fucking idiot. I'm quiet because I'm stupid, and I like to cause trouble. It's what I know how to do. It's what I've done a million times before.

This time is different, though. I always knew what I was doing before. I don't know what I'm doing now. I don't know how to talk to her. I don't know how to tell her anything. Close my eyes and just do it? Nah, it's not that easy.

I say something else instead. It's probably pretty fucking dumb, too. I shouldn't say this shit.

"I had a crush on you when I was younger, Ashley."

"When?" she asks.

I don't answer her. It's too difficult of a question.

"I had a crush on you, too," she says.

"That's the thing, though," I say. "We're not good for each other. I know it, and I think you know it, too. Even if you weren't my stepsister, I'm not good for you. You understand, right? You need to find a nice guy who can be everything for you. That's not me. That's never going to be me."

We're quiet after that. I think that's it. Maybe she fell asleep. I'm tired, too. I close my eyes.

"I think you underestimate yourself," she says. "I don't think you're as bad as you think you are."

"Not now," I say, whispering. "I can be as good as I want for a week or two, Princess, but that's it. That's what always gets me in trouble."

"I know," she mumbles. She's falling asleep on me. "I know more about you than you might think."

It's quiet again. Longer now. She falls asleep, breathing softly on my chest. I sneak a quick kiss, and she puckers up her lips, trying to kiss me back in her sleep.

"I know a lot about you, too, Ashley," I whisper before I close my eyes and try to go to sleep.

6 - Ashley

MY ALARM GOES OFF on my phone and I jolt up out of bed. Oh no, I'm going to miss my class, I have to get up, I have to get ready, what time is it, what...

Oh, wait. A sleepy looking Ethan grumbles and rolls away from me. He looks really cute when he's tired. I sink back down into bed and wrap my arms around him, then kiss his face. My nose nuzzles against his and he bats me away softly, pushing me with his hands.

"What the fuck?" he says. "What time is it?"

"Um..." I check my phone, even though I don't have to. I know what time I set my alarm for. "Six," I say.

"Who the fuck wakes up at six in the morning?" he asks.

"Did you forget the plan?" I ask him.

"Nah," he says. "I just want to go back to bed."

"What if I want you to wake up?" I ask. "What if I want to give you a morning blowjob?"

"You know what, Princess? I think you should always follow your heart's desires. That shit will never steer you wrong."

I laugh and hug him and kiss him. He grumbles, but squeezes me tight in his arms, too.

"Man, I got a raw deal here," he says. "Now I'm awake, but there's no morning blowjob. What's up with that?"

"Maybe we can cuddle first?" I ask.

"Yeah, maybe," he says, grinning. "Come here."

I don't have anywhere to go; I'm already as close as possible. He squeezes me tighter in his arms, then lets me loose.

"Maybe we should wake up now and go make breakfast?" I ask. "Then we can go hang out for the day? At the beach, or we could go to a park. Ooh, we could go to an amusement park and ride the rollercoasters, or we could go hiking, or..."

"Whoa whoa whoa, calm down," Ethan says. "I'm not awake enough for this conversation. You want to hang out today?"

"Do you?" I ask. Maybe I'm getting too far ahead of myself.

"Yeah, that sounds cool," he says. "Alright, I'll get up."

He stumbles up and practically falls off the bed, but catches himself and stands. Groggy and disoriented, Ethan heads towards the bathroom.

"Where are you going?" I ask.

"I'm going to take a shower, Princess. Just give me a bit."

"I can join you?" I offer.

"Listen, if you come in that shower with me, we're never going to get out of the house. You do what you want, though. Don't say I didn't warn you."

I giggle, and he turns to look at me, smirking.

"Yeah, exactly," he says. "Your choice. Give me ten minutes to myself so we can hang out today, or come in and make me do something we might regret."

I don't think I'd regret it. I do want to hang out with him, though. I like having sex with Ethan, but... I want to do more, too. We *have* been doing more, but it's easier when you're alone, isn't it? With our parents here, that kind of hinders our at-home options. Going out will be nice, though. Hiking could be fun. In the middle of the woods, just us, all alone. Hm...

I decide to leave him alone for a little while, but I also decide to not leave him alone. I snatch up my phone and lay back in bed, then tap and swipe to bring up the menu for texting. I start writing one to Ethan, one that he'll get as soon as he checks his phone. I wonder when he'll see it? It's fun to guess.

This is what I text him:

Ethan, I can't wait to give you a blowjob later. Maybe I'll come into the shower right now and give you one. How naughty would that be? Giving my brother a blowjob in the shower while our parents are sleeping right downstairs? Would you like that? Text me back when you get this and tell me what you want to do to me, too.

I send that message to him. And then, for good measure, I pull down the covers and take a picture of myself. Naked, of course, from the head down, while I'm laying there, so that Ethan can see what I see, the top of my body, my breasts, slowly heading towards my sex, my legs, and then the tops of my toes. I send that to him, too.

Maybe that last one is a bad idea. I've never sent anyone a picture like that before. To be fair, I haven't done a lot of things before, but I've been breaking new ground with Ethan for days, so why not?

Less than a minute later, I get a text back. Oh, wow. Did he bring his phone with him into the bathroom? That doesn't seem safe. I can hear him in the shower...

I tap to read the text, and then my heart stops. How did that happen? I must have misclicked. I didn't text Ethan. This is definitely not Ethan.

It's Jake. My ex-boyfriend.

I knew you were desperate for affection when I started dating you, Ashley, but I didn't think you'd go so far as to sleep with your brother. Nice pic, though. You always did have a hot body.

Oh my God oh my God oh my God. I text him back, fast.

That was just a joke, Jake. I wanted to annoy you because you were such a jerk to me. I'm done with you. I never want to talk to you again. Leave me alone.

He writes back almost immediately.

Yeah? How about I forward these messages to your parents. I wonder what they'd think. Should I send them the nude pic, too?

I furiously tap on the screen to text him back, but then I give up. This won't work. I tap to call him instead. He picks up after one ring.

"You wouldn't dare," I say. No hello, just straight to the point.

"Hey," he says. "I *would* dare. Apparently you don't know me very well."

"Of course I don't," I say. "I thought you were nice, and then you had sex with me and broke up with me right before we went on summer break? Who does that?"

"You kept holding out on me," he says. "That's the only reason I stayed with you so long, but it was getting old, Ashley. Now I guess I know why. You're giving it up to you brother."

"He's my stepbrother," I say, as if this makes it any better. "It's not illegal or anything. What do you care?"

"I'm recording this conversation, too. Thanks for admitting that you had sex with your brother. Makes it easier for me."

I clench my jaw and glare into the phone. "Seriously, what do you want? Just leave me alone."

"I wanted you to stop being such a prude when I was with you, but that barely ever happened. We had sex like... what, twice? In two months? That's not normal, Ashley."

"You never wanted to cuddle with me," I tell him. "You never wanted to do anything with me. You always just tried to get in my pants, even when I told you to stop. And when we had sex, you just left right after."

"I didn't want to date you in the first place. It was a bet. That I won, of course. You were alright in bed, so I thought I'd keep trying and get my money's worth, but that never worked."

"I'm hanging up now," I say. "Seriously, I never want to talk to you again. Don't try to talk to--"

"Don't you fucking dare hang up, you bitch," he says, startling me. Is this really Jake? I feel like I always kind of knew he wasn't nice. Maybe this is why I was reluctant to do anything with him. He never treated me like... like a person? Like a girlfriend? It's obvious looking back on it, but at the time I just kind of wanted someone to...

I wanted someone to love me. I wanted to love someone, too. I don't know how I could be so naive.

"Here's how this is going to go," he says. "I was just going to give up on you, but you've given me a golden opportunity now. I know your family's rich, so don't try to get out of this, either. I want you to fly to me tomorrow morning. I don't care what you have to tell your mom and dad or brother. Tell them you're going to visit a friend. You're going to stay with me for the rest of the weekend, then you can go back home."

I scrunch up my nose and make a face into the phone, for all the good it does me. "Why would I do that? I'm not doing that."

"You're going to do it or else I'm telling your parents everything," he says. "I'm telling everyone at school, too. I'll send them the text messages, the picture, and these phone recordings. What do you think people will think of you after they find out you're fucking your brother, Ashley?"

"I..." How could this have happened? I didn't ever mean for this to happen.

It's wrong. Not just this, but everything. I knew it was wrong, but I thought I could get away with it. Why, though? I'm not like this. I'm good. I'm the good girl, the girl with perfect grades, the girl who does everything right, prim and proper. I don't cause trouble, I don't get into trouble, I don't...

I'm in trouble now, though. The first time I ever stray from my Little Miss Perfect image, and this happens? I never wanted to be Little Miss Perfect to begin with. No one ever says it in a nice way. Except for Ethan. It's cute and playful when he says it. He's the only one who... who what?

I'm so confused. I don't understand.

"Just come here tomorrow, be my sex toy for a couple of days, and you can go back home," Jake says, almost sweetly. "Everything will be fine. For now, at least. I might change my mind in a couple weeks. I might need more incentive not to tell your little secret, Ashley. I'll let you know, though. You can make me forget all about it by coming for a visit for a few days ago. When we're back in college, it'll be even easier. It'll be our little secret, as long as you do what I say."

"Jake," I whisper. "You can't tell anyone."

"I won't, as long as you come here tomorrow. I'm not playing around here, Ashley. I mean it. I can't wait to fuck you as much as I want for the next few days. I've wanted to do it for a long time, but you're too stuck up and prude. Never would have thought you had a secret like this, though."

I open my mouth to start to say something, but he says more first.

"Hope you don't mind, but I'm going to have to make you wash out your pussy a few times before we start. It's honestly more than a little gross that you've been having sex with your brother.

That's just disgusting. What's next? A pack of dogs? You sick bitch."

I tremble and shake. I can't believe he's saying this. But I sort of agree, too. I don't know how to disagree with him. It is. It's wrong. I knew it was wrong, but I got swept away, and I never thought anyone would find out, and...

And now I've ruined all of it. I ruined everything. I should have stopped yesterday. I could have. Ethan gave me the chance. This is my fault. It's all my fault.

I hear the water turn off in the bathroom. He's out of the shower now, probably drying off at this very moment.

"Tomorrow," Jake says. "I'll text you the information, and I'll even meet you at the airport. Be here by the afternoon, or else. Don't do anything you'll regret, Ashley. Anything more than what you've already done, at least. You dirty whore."

He hangs up. The phone clicks off, ending the call. I hold it to my ear, listless, confused, and hurt.

How could this happen? What did I do? Why did I do that?

7 - Ethan

WHEN I FINISH MY SHOWER, I dry off and get dressed, then step back into my room. I smile, cocky and arrogant, ready to tease Ashley, but she's...

What the fuck, she's gone? Where did she go? Her clothes are gone, too. Not that she was wearing them, but I saw them on the floor when I got up this morning, so I know she brought them. From the looks of it, her cellphone is gone, too.

She must have gone back to her room. Yeah, well, I think I'll pay her a visit. Couldn't hurt.

I step into the hall and walk towards her room. The door's closed. I try to open it, but it's locked, too.

I knock. "Hey, you in there?" I ask.

"Go away, Ethan," she says.

"What's with the attitude?"

"I said go away!" she screeches.

"Holy fuck, are you serious? What the fuck is wrong with you? Did I do something to piss you off or what?"

"I..." She falters and chokes. "Please, Ethan. I don't feel good right now. I want to be left alone. Please?" By the end, she sounds like she's begging.

"It's cool, Princess," I say. "Are you sick or something?"

Oh shit. Sick? In the morning? Morning sickness? Wait, nah. I'm no doctor, but I'm pretty sure a girl can't get pregnant that fast. That'd be some fucked up shit, though. Also, she's on birth control. Should be fine. Maybe I'm potent as fuck, though. Kind of impressive if that's the case. And fucked up. I need to stop thinking this stupid shit, especially because I know it can't be true.

She doesn't say anything. I can hear something, but it's hard to tell what it is. Is she crying? I've heard girls cry plenty of times, and I've made them cry most of those times, but I didn't even think I did anything this time. Maybe I'm becoming more of an asshole without realizing it? Fuck.

"I'm going to go make breakfast," I say. "Pancakes, alright? Just how you like them. I won't bug you about it. Let's just hang out and have some food. If you aren't feeling good, we can stay home today. I'll go get you some soup and we can watch movies on Netflix. Sound good?"

She doesn't say anything. I'm not sure what to say now. I'm not good at this. I've never had to convince a girl to spend time with me before. It's strange. A lot harder than it sounds, too. Who knew this shit was difficult? I feel bad for the guys that are less fortunate than me.

Not that I do anything good with my super-powers here. I'm basically just a dick. Sorry?

Yeah, well, one more try, alright? Let's see how this goes.

"I'll bring it up for you," I say. "Breakfast in bed, alright? You get in your pajamas, get cozy under the blankets, and I'll bring you some pan-cakes on a platter in a few. Don't you worry. I got this."

I hear her sniffling through the door, but she's not crying anymore. Then she gets up. Is she going to open the door? I hope so. But, nah, she goes into her bathroom instead. Must have grabbed a tissue, because a second later I hear her blow her nose.

Shit. I feel bad. How'd she get sick? She seemed fine before I got in the shower. Maybe she just needs more sleep. I get cranky when I don't have enough sleep, too. Yeah, fuck, it's six-thirty now, isn't it? Who the fuck wakes up this early?

I used to. For football. Practice during the summer started at seven during high school, so I'd wake up at five, eat breakfast, head over to the school, and be dressed and ready on the field by seven. It was fun. I love football. I don't miss waking up at five in the fucking morning, though. That shit's rough.

Anyways, no time to worry or think about this. I've got to go make my Princess pancakes. Real fucking special, too. I'm going all out here. Chocolate chips. Aw yeah. Damn, I'm good at this.

8 - Ashley

DON'T KNOW WHAT TO DO. I don't know if there's anything I can do. This entire situation is beyond me. I'm in too deep and I'm drowning and that's it. It's done. I'm done.

Maybe I can pretend none of this ever happened. Maybe it didn't? It might have all been just a dream. If I go to sleep, take a nap, and wake up, I'll realize that every little part of this was a figment of my imagination. It's not a crime to fantasize about sleeping with your stepbrother, right? It's not actually a crime to sleep with your stepbrother either, though. I'm not sure that logic is going to work for me right now.

I can lie, though. I can say it's wrong. I can refuse to go and if Jake really does tell my parents, then I'll just say he's the one that's lying. Who are they going to believe, me or him? I'd like to think they'll believe me, but Jake has pretty damning evidence to the contrary. Why did I even take that picture of myself naked? That was a stupid idea. Stupid, stupid stupid!

For someone who's supposed to be smart, I'm not sure how I could do something so dumb. This entire situation is dumb, though.

No, it's not. It's not dumb. I've been having a nice time. I really enjoy hanging out with Ethan. He's nice. He wouldn't blackmail me like this, even if we're only doing this for a week. If he was the one who had gotten the picture instead of Jake, he never would have told anyone or shown anyone. This is what I want to believe, but I know Ethan, too. He's not exactly a saint. I feel like he still has some sense of decency, though. I know he does.

My options right now are that I can pretend none of this ever happened, or... I can admit that it did. I can accept the fact that Jake has a hold over me, that I accidentally gave it to him, and I can deal with it.

How? By going and doing what he wants me to do. Is it worth it, though?

If I do, I know it'll hurt. I know it's wrong. I don't want to be some object for him to use for his own sexual gratification. That's never what I wanted.

I know that sounds strange, because it seems like maybe that's what Ethan and I have been doing for the past few days, but it's not. We've been having fun, too. He's taught me things that I don't know if anyone else could have taught me. He's shown me that things I thought were wrong aren't actually bad when they happen between two people who care about each other, and he's given me a reason to want to find someone who can treat me...

...just like he does.

That's it, isn't it? Ethan has set the bar for me, given me expectations and an understanding of myself that I never really understood before, and that's it. I don't know if that's a good thing or a bad thing. It makes me want to find someone like him, or someone better, but I don't know if there is anyone better.

Why can't I just have him? I know it's not that easy. Life isn't that easy, and our situation isn't that easy. Nothing is easy. Why does this have to be so difficult, though? It hurts.

I want to remember, though. I want to remember every part of what happened between us. I don't want to forget it. I don't want anyone to tell me it's bad or wrong or that we shouldn't have done that. Deep down I know we shouldn't have, but I'm also very thankful that we did. I would rather cherish the memories from the past few days than to let them become tainted with unwanted criticism and disgusted looks from everyone around me.

And so I only have one option, don't I? If I don't want anyone else to know, I have to do what Jake wants me to do. That's the only way. It's the only thing I can think of. Either that, or somehow invent a time machine, go back, and stop myself from ever mistakenly texting my ex-boyfriend in the first place.

I should have deleted his number from my phone when we broke up that day. I was holding out hope before, though. I thought he might change his mind, that he'd text me and apologize, but then things happened with Ethan and I forgot all about that.

I don't want Jake to text me now. I never want to speak with him again. I guess I have to, though. I guess I'm going to secretly buy a plane ticket and go see him tomorrow.

It's only a few days, right? That's what I thought when Ethan and I started our stepbrother with benefits situation, too, though. Apparently a few days can be a long time. A few days can change your entire life.

Someone knocks on my door. I ignore them and bury my face in my pillow. I hope they go away. I hope everyone goes away. I can't deal with this right now. I feel physically ill. My stomach hurts. I want to be left alone.

"Hey, open up," Ethan says.

Go away, Ethan. I think this, but I don't say it.

He waits for a few seconds, then knocks again. "Wow, I make you pancakes and deliver them and everything and you're not even going to open the door? I see how it is."

"I don't feel good!" I say, shouting at the door.

"Yeah, I get it. That's why I brought them up here for you!" Ethan says, shouting back.

Someone's going to hear him. Or me. They'll hear one of us. I don't know why he won't listen. He's never listened to anyone in his entire life, though, has he? That's part of who he is. That's part of why he's trouble. I know exactly why Ethan Colton has a reputation as a bad boy. He's being bad right now even if it looks like he's trying to be nice.

"They're chocolate chip, Ashley," he says, pounding on my bedroom door again. "Real fucking melty chocolate, too. More chocolate chips than any one person should ever eat for breakfast. These things are smothered in chocolate."

Chocolate chip pancakes? I wish he hadn't done that. I wish I couldn't imagine mouthfuls of fluffy pancakes and melted chocolate right now. He's making this too difficult for me.

"What about the syrup?" I ask him. If he forgot the syrup, I can fight this. I have some semblance of willpower left. I really do.

"Yeah, I've got it right here," he says. "The whole fucking jug, just for you. Use the entire thing. I don't care. You're the one who's sick."

I'm not actually sick. Not in the way he thinks. My heart is sick, but I don't know if that counts.

I roll my way off the bed and stand up, then rush to the door. When I open it, Ethan is standing there. There's nothing in his hands.

"You lied to me!" I say, making a face at him. "I thought you made pancakes, but you lied. I can't believe you did that. I hate--"

He claps a hand over my mouth. "Stop right there, Princess. Close your mouth for a second and look down."

I push his hand away and glare at him, but I look down, too. There's... Oh wow.

On a small tray stand, like the ones that people use for breakfast in bed, which I suppose is what this is, there's a plate of pancakes just as chocolatey and melty as Ethan said. Next to that there's the grey jug of fresh maple syrup, plus forks and knives, and another plate with sausage on it. To the side are two empty glasses and a half gallon carton of orange juice.

"That's too many pancakes," I tell him. "I can't eat all of those."

"Greedy much?" he asks, narrowing his eyes at me. "You going to share some with me or what?"

"There's only one plate," I say.

"So what? There's two forks and two knives. I think we can share. I swear I don't have cooties, Princess."

"Cooties," I say, rolling my eyes. "Are we in second grade again?"

"Might as well be. Who the fuck locks someone out of their room like that and refuses to answer the door?"

"Um, you?" I say. "I"m pretty sure you've done it plenty of times before."

"Yeah yeah, let me do that over," he says. "You're the good girl here, Princess. You're supposed to be polite and nice and shit. Why are you being a bitch?"

"Did you just call me a bitch?" I ask, trying not to laugh. The way he said it sounded funny, though. Maybe I should be offended, but I'm not.

"If the shoe fits," he says. Ethan glances down at my feet. "Fuck, I guess it doesn't. You're not wearing any. Sorry about that. You mind putting some shoes on so I can call you a bitch again?"

I stick my tongue out at him and make a face, but he stops me. He stops me by putting his hands on my hips and pulling me close, then touching the tip of his nose to mine.

"Did I do something to make you upset?" he asks, hushed. "When I came out of the shower you were gone. Are you alright?"

I blush. We're close. This is too close, and he's holding me too close. What if someone sees us? What if my mom or his dad comes upstairs and they see us like this? What then?

I like it, though. I like how he's worried, and how he's holding me like he cares. It's cute and sweet even though I can feel the telltale signs of his erection poking at my stomach. Ethan Colton only has a certain amount of sweetness in him; the rest of him is raw sex and arrogance.

"You have an erection," I tell him, wrinkling my nose.

"Holy fuck, I'm trying to be slightly less of an asshole right now. Did you really have to point that out?"

I laugh, then I kiss him quick and slip away from him. "Yes," I say. "I did. And it's not you. You didn't do anything. I just don't feel very well right now. I don't want to... I don't want to have sex, Ethan. Not today. Please."

"I get that I have a raging hard-on that probably almost broke one of your ribs, but I came up here to have breakfast with you, Princess. Nothing else. If I had ulterior motives, I'd just tell you straight up."

"If that's really why you came, then you can come in," I say. "I accept your breakfast proposal."

"Way to make it sound dirty," he says.

I don't understand what he means at first, but then, um... proposal, proposition, propositioning for sex? I feel like chocolate chip pancakes are a pretty good bargaining chip for something like that, too. Especially Ethan's pancakes. If this were any other time, I'd probably gladly indulge in some indecent proposal in exchange for this meal...

Not now, though. Probably not ever again. We need to stop.

That doesn't mean I need to reject him completely, though. Does it? I think it probably does, but I don't want it to.

"Go lay down," Ethan says, smacking my butt. "Get in bed, Princess. You need to rest up and get better. Who the fuck gets sick their first week of summer break? That's bullshit."

I jump up and spin around, glaring at him. "You just spanked me!" I say.

"Better get back in bed quick before I do it again!" he says, staring hard at me.

I roll my eyes and slowly walk towards the bed, sashaying my hips side to side. Ethan goes to spank me again, but I see him out of the corner of my eye and I dodge and jump away, then scamper fast to the bed. I sneak under the covers and wait for him to join me.

He bends down to grab the food tray, then hefts it up and brings it over. He sits it above my lap, pulling the legs of the tray out so it's more like a table. I sit with my back against the headboard, a pillow propping me up. Ethan goes to close the door.

"Locked?" he asks.

"Why?" I ask. "If you aren't planning on um... seducing me, then I think it's fine to leave it unlocked."

He shrugs. "Have it your way, Princess."

I realize why it might be better to have it locked a few seconds after he closes the door and steps further into my room, though. I'm in pajamas, sitting under my blankets, and Ethan's in pajamas, too. He's about to join me on the bed. Even though this isn't exactly supposed to be sexual, if our parents come up and see us like this, um...

I don't know. I don't want to know. It's still early. They probably aren't awake yet. It'll probably be fine.

I kind of want to lay in bed with Ethan, too. I kind of wish I could cuddle with him. I wish I could tell him about what happened, about what Jake said, about the trouble I'm in, and I wish he could help me.

He can't, though. I know that. This is all my fault.

Ethan goes to the wall opposite my bed and flips on the TV, then snatches up the remote and brings it over to me. He sits in the bed, above the covers, leaning back against the headboard just like I am. We're close, but separate, too; there are blankets and the legs of a breakfast-in-bed tray separating us.

He toys around with the remote until he brings up our family shared Netflix account. We each have special profiles to keep ourselves separate. His finger hovers over the selector. He's going to pick his profile, or that's what it looks like, but at the last minute he switches to mine.

"What are you doing?" I ask. "Are you snooping on my Netflix profile?"

"Nah," he says. "I've already snooped on it before. You need to watch some better shows. What's with all the girly shit?"

"Um, I'm a girl, Ethan. Have you not realized this? I thought you would have figured it out by now, especially considering the last couple of days."

"Holy fuck, you're a girl?" he says, eyes wide. "No fucking way. Tell me more, Princess."

"You're so dumb," I say, giggling.

"Yeah, well, I get that a lot," he says, grinning at me. "I need a study buddy or some shit. Maybe one who can help me over Skype. All the girls I ask to come help me study think I just want to fuck them. What's up with that?"

"And how many girls have you asked to help you study?" I ask, glancing over and narrowing my eyes.

"None," he says. "Not yet, anyways. There's this really sexy chick who asked me recently, though. I've kind of got a thing for her, but she's off limits. She said she'd help me, and if I did we could fool around with video chat after. You think I should take her up on it?"

"What kind of *thing* do you have for her?" I ask him.

"Nothing serious, Princess. Don't worry. You're still my number one."

"What's that supposed to mean?" I ask. "I thought we had rules..."

"Yeah," he says. "I meant like... you're my stepsister, right? We're like family or something. I got your back, yo."

"Oh," I say, then I scrunch up my brow. "Did you just say 'yo' to me? Who says that?"

He shrugs. "No clue. It seemed appropriate at the time. You think I was laying it on too thick?"

"I don't know," I say, but I'm not exactly answering his question. I pause for a second. Should I ask him? Yes, I decide to. "Ethan, if you weren't my stepbrother, would you date me?"

"Huh? Where'd that come from?"

"I just... am I the kind of girl that a guy wants to date? Or am I just the kind of girl that guys sleep with while they're looking for someone better?"

"You think there's someone better than you?" he asks.

"I don't know. Probably, right?"

"Nah," he says. "Listen, Princess, this is how it is. I know all about this. I'll tell you, alright?"

"Alright," I say.

"Every girl is perfect. Each and every single one of them. There's never going to be anyone better than you, because you're already perfect. Got it?"

"I'm definitely not perfect," I tell him.

"Nah," he says. "You are. You just don't realize it yet. That's the thing, though. It's hard to figure this shit out. You can't do it on your own. You need some help. When you find the right guy for you, you'll know it. You'll just wake up someday and realize that you're perfect, and you know what? That's all because of you, because you're perfect, and you found someone to be perfect with. The guy's probably going to be some random dude, but he'll be cool, too. It's fine if he's kind of screwy, because he'll have some other positive qualities, like letting you know you're perfect."

"You're refusing to answer my question on purpose, aren't you?" I ask, smiling. "You're going off on a tangent!"

"Maybe," he says, grinning. "The point of the matter here is that you're the kind of girl every guy wants to date, but they don't always realize it at first. Any guy who would sleep with you just because he's got a dick is basically just a dick, and you don't want to spend time with someone like that. He can't see a good thing even when she's right in front of him and he's got his cock inside her, up close and personal."

"Except you, of course," I say. "You're the exception, huh?"

"Nah, I'm no exception, Princess. I know a good thing when I see it. I know that girls like you deserve guys a million times better than me, though. You'll find him some day, too. You'll bring him home, and I'll meet him, and I'll shake his hand and say 'Fuck you. You ever hurt my sister and I'll beat your fucking face in.' It'll be real sweet and romantic like that."

"Oh, it sounds great," I say, laughing. "I'm sure he'll love meeting you. I can't wait."

"If he's cool enough, I'll show him how to make good pancakes, too," Ethan says. "Maybe. Maybe I'll just keep that shit for myself. Need to have a trump card to knock him down a peg if he tries to one up me, right?"

I stick my tongue out at him and laugh. Ethan slices a piece of pancake away quick and smears it in the melted chocolate coating our shared plate, then he stuffs it in my mouth before I realize it. I glare at him, but then I taste it, and... Oh my God this is amazing. It's so good! I want to eat these every day for the rest of my life. That's probably not very healthy, but I'd exercise extra to make up for it.

I chew and swallow, living in heaven for every single second of it.

Ethan smiles, watching me. "Good?" he asks.

"Very good," I say. "What about you?"

"Haven't tried them yet. We still need syrup. Add as much as you want. I'll pour us some juice."

"Alright," I say. "But um... Ethan?"

"Yeah, what's up?"

"I didn't mean that. I... I meant when are you going to find your perfect girl? Do you know?"

"Nah," he says. "Relationships aren't for me, Princess. I'm just a cocky prick."

"Maybe someday you'll find her," I say. "Maybe?"

"Yeah, maybe," he says with a shrug. "Maybe I already found her and I fucked it up. I wouldn't be surprised."

"If you did, you could tell her," I say. "I bet she would accept your apology if you said you were sorry."

"I don't say sorry, Princess. Not sure if you've realized that yet. I'm too stubborn. I do things my way. If she doesn't want to go along with it, she can go fuck herself."

"Maybe she will!" I say, laughing. "And she'll send you a picture of it, and say 'You see what you're missing, Ethan? Stop being such a jerk and come over here. I'm tired of fucking myself. You do it for me.' It could happen."

"Whoa! Did Little Miss Perfect just swear? Holy fuck."

"I did not!" I say, protesting. "It's just a verb. I was using it as a verb, which is acceptable."

"I feel like we've had this conversation before," he says.

"Me too. Do you remember who won last time?"

"Fuck if I know. You're the smart one. You should remember."

"Smart people don't always have good memories," I say, rolling my eyes at him. "If it's up to me, I'm going to say that I won, though. I'm still Little Miss Perfect and a good girl."

"Good," Ethan says, smiling. "Now eat your damn breakfast before it gets cold. Where's the maple syrup? Seriously, Princess, I give you one job. Just one job! What's up with that?"

"You need to calm yourself down, Ethan Colton!" I say, snatching up the syrup jug and waving it at him like a weapon. "Patience!"

"Yeah yeah. Whatever you say," he says. "Hey, what are we watching?"

"I don't know. You pick something," I say, pouring syrup onto our pancakes.

"No idea why I clicked on your Netflix profile, then," he says, grumbling.

"Pick something from my watch list. I have a lot on there."

"It's all dumb girly shit, isn't it?" he asks, clicking through to check it out. "Oh wait. Whoa. Sons of Anarchy? You got a naughty streak or something?"

"Wouldn't you like to know?" I ask.

"Twenty bucks says I probably already do."

"Is that a bet?"

"Nah, you don't want to bet with me, Princess. I play to win."

We start watching the first episode of the series while sitting in bed and eating pancakes together. The sausage, too. Plus orange juice. Everything is good. It's really good. When we're finished, I pick up the tray and put it on the floor next to my bed.

Now it's just us. Ethan and I, laying in bed together, side by side. I'm cuddled under the blankets and he's laying above them, but we're still really close. He inches a little closer to me and we lay our heads on the same pillow. He puts his hand by my leg, and I move my hand under the covers closer to his. I touch his hand with my fingers, sort of. I'm beneath the blankets and he's above them, but that's alright. This is fine, right? It's not bad to do this. No one can ever see it, anyways. It's hidden from everyone. No one will ever know.

Ethan teases the palm of my hand with his finger, tracing patterns on me above the blanket. Then he reaches over and squeezes my thigh quick, fingers gripping my leg through the covers. I nudge my head against his, and he nudges me back.

"I'll go get soup later, alright? What's wrong with you? You want some cold medicine or something?"

"Just soup would be nice," I say. "Will you have some, too? Can we stay up here and have it?"

"Yeah, sure, why not?" he asks. "Sounds good. Don't worry, I'll take care of you, Princess. You'll feel better in no time. Then we'll go to the beach or something."

I wish that were true. I'm not sure if I'll feel better or not. I want to believe him, though.

A NOTE FROM MIA

Uh oh...

There's one more book after this one, and it's going to be quite a powerful one, I think. These books with Ethan and Ashley are supposed to be a fun and exciting romantic comedy, but sometimes you need a little thrill to keep life interesting, don't you think? And, um... well, Ashley certainly got that in this one!

She's a good girl, and Ethan brought her out of her comfort zone, but she's not exactly up to being completely naughty yet. Also, she needs to be more careful with text messages! Naughty pictures? Eek.

I think that would have been sexy if Ethan got them, though. What do you think he would have done? Something that the both of them would have enjoyed, no doubt. Haha.

This is really difficult, though. It's not just her parents that she has to worry about now, but everyone else, too. And I think what's worse about that is that her and Ethan go to completely different schools. That's kind of hard to deal with, if you don't really have friends and your ex-boyfriend is hellbent on making your life terrible.

I think she can work through it, though. I don't think she can do it on her own, but I think that she's learned a lot these past few days and I think she can do it with a little help. From... who?

You'll find out soon! It's a good next book, I promise.

If you like these books, I'd love if you rated and reviewed them. Do you think that Ashley will be able to make it through this? Is she going to have to tell her parents, or can she figure out a way to keep her secret. Even if she does, what about her and Ethan? Are they going to be together for the rest of the week still, or longer, or is this it for them? Is she going to tell him about Jake and her mistake, too? Too many questions, but they all get answered soon!

I hope you're liking this series so far. It's been a lot of fun.

Thanks for reading, and I'll see you soon! (next book!)

~MIA

ABOUT THE AUTHOR

Mia likes to have fun in all aspects of her life. Whether she's out enjoying the beautiful weather or spending time at home reading a book, a smile is never far from her face. She's prone to randomly laughing at nothing in particular except for whatever idea amuses her at any given moment.

Sometimes you just need to enjoy life, right?

She loves to read, dance, and explore outdoors. Chamomile tea and bubble baths are two of her favorite things. Flowers are especially nice, and she could get lost in a garden if it's big enough and no one's around to remind her that there are other things to do.

She lives in New Hampshire, where the weather is beautiful and the autumn colors are amazing.

Manufactured by Amazon.ca
Bolton, ON